Design Coordinator, English-language
edition: Miko McGinty

Library of Congress Cataloging-in-Publication Data
Brouillard, Anne.
  [Bain de la Cantatrice. English]
  The bathtub prima donna / written and illustrated by Anne
Brouillard.
      p. cm.
  Summary: A self-absorbed songstress uses her voice to
tickle the clouds into raining for her bath, but in the process
a nearby village becomes flooded.
  ISBN 0-8109-4093-0
  [1. Singing—Fiction. 2. Baths—Fiction. 3. Rain and rainfall—
Fiction.] I. Title
PZ7.B79975Bat 1999
[E]—dc21   98-53970

Harry N. Abrams, Inc.
100 Fifth Avenue
New York, N.Y. 10011
www.abramsbooks.com

The Bathtub Prima Donna

Anne Brouillard

Harry N. Abrams, Inc., Publishers

When Prima Donna woke it was a beautiful day.
That is what she ordered and she always had her way.

Prima Donna sang of meadows glistening with dew.
She sang to greet the morning, as Prima Donnas do.

She sang as she rose from her bed and to her bath she went.
She sang as she turned the knobs, but alas no water was sent.

"Ooh, no! What is this? No water!" she shrilled.
She pleaded, she begged—but the pipes refused to yield.

"How will I find water without a rain cloud in the sky? I must sing to please the clouds. Yes, I'll give it a try.

What shall I sing? How shall I set the rain free? I'll sing of gushing torrents, and floods from sea to sea!"

Practicing as she went, she climbed the highest hill. She paused and took a deep breath, and then began to trill:

"La-la-la-la-la, la-la-la-la-la . . .

"A little village slept in the hollow of a vale, free from the rages of wind, storm, and gale."

The good folk who lived there had worry not one.
They spent their days in the warmth of the sun.

"Then over the village a storm cloud grew and soon became a dark, simmering brew.

So drop, drop, drop the rain did fall and the people scattered to house and hall.

"Rain fell on the churches, the houses, the gates,

down it came gushing and stopped up the grates.

"The water rose up to swirl at the doors,

then climbed even further to cover the floors.

"Cried the townsfolk, 'When ever will it stop?

We cannot bear to see another drop!'

"In the hollow of the vale, a puddle became a sea,
and all the villagers were forced to pack and flee.

They quickly fled the village to seek a drier shore while the waters swelled up to an even higher score."

 Prima Donna paused. A raindrop splashed her head!

"The clouds are pleased, indeed!
Bath time!" Prima Donna said.

From sea to bubbly sea she floated on her back.

Perhaps she'll sing a new song—
what else does Prima Donna lack?